LITTLE MISS BAD

Roger Hargreaves

Written and illustrated by
Adam Hargreaves

Little Miss Sunshine looked out of the window and thought back on all the things that had happened in the last week.

Lots of things.

Lots of bad things.

Some things were just a little bit bad.

Mr Uppity's tennis racquet strings were swapped for spaghetti.

And the cream in Mr Greedy's cream buns was replaced with toothpaste.

Some things were really quite bad.

Little Miss Splendid's shower had covered her with ink.

And someone had painted cracks on the walls of Mr Worry's house.

Mr Worry was so worried that his house might fall down, he had moved into his garden shed.

Some things were really very bad indeed!

Someone had sawn Mr Forgetful's car in half.
Fortunately, Mr Forgetful did not get upset.
He simply thought that he must have forgotten the
other half and left it at home.

And someone had sneaked into Little Miss Neat's house while she was away on holiday and left all the taps running.

Little Miss Neat did get upset.

Nobody knew who had done all these things, but Little Miss Sunshine had a very good idea who was behind it all.

"Little Miss Bad," she murmured to herself.

Little Miss Bad was not good.

Far from it.

In fact, about as far as you can get, which is a long way.

But how to catch Little Miss Bad? This was the question that Little Miss Sunshine was turning over in her mind.

And then she had an idea.

A very clever idea.

The next day a poster appeared in the Town Square. It announced that there was to be a 'Grand Competition' to discover the most mischievous, naughty or bad trick that had been played in the last week. First prize was a fabulous holiday.

"How easy," said Little Miss Bad to herself. "That holiday is as good as mine."

The day of the Grand Competition dawned.
By midday a large crowd had gathered in the Town Square. A stage had been built in the middle of the square.

Little Miss Sunshine called for quiet.

"Each contestant," she explained, "will come up on stage and describe their entry and then the panel of judges will decide upon a winner. First up is Little Miss Bad!"

Little Miss Bad could not wait to get on stage.

She was so excited.

She had spent all the previous night trying to pick her worst or best trick, depending on how you looked at it, but she had not been able to decide.

So she described them all to the crowd. From Mr Uppity's tennis racquet strings all the way through to Little Miss Neat's wet house.

She described them in great detail.

Little Miss Bad was so carried away she failed to notice that the crowd had fallen silent. It was only when she had finished that she saw the expressions on everyone's faces.

She looked to Little Miss Sunshine, who was the only person in the square with a smile on her face, a rather smug smile, and it suddenly occurred to Little Miss Bad just what she had been tricked into doing.

"I-I-I was only j-j-joking," she stammered.

"Anything more to say?" said Little Miss Sunshine.

Little Miss Bad looked very ashamed. "I'm sorry," she said.

Little Miss Bad had learnt her lesson that day.

The lesson continued for a number of weeks as it took her a long time to repair all the damage and clean Little Miss Neat's house.

Mr Forgetful's car will never look quite the same. Luckily he can't remember what it looked like in the first place.

But nothing she had to do was half as bad as those moments standing on the stage with the crowd glaring at her.

It was a very long time before she even thought of doing anything bad.

And the same could be said of one other person that day.

Mr Mischief.

Who slipped away from his place next to the stage and slunk off home, where he breathed a very deep sigh of relief!

3 Great Offers for MR.MEN Fans!

MR.MEN TOKEN

1 New Mr. Men or Little Miss Library Bus Presentation Cases

A brand new stronger, roomier school bus library box, with sturdy carrying handle and stay-closed fasteners.

The full colour, wipe-clean boxes make a great home for your full collection.

They're just £5.99 inc P&P and free bookmark!

☐ MR. MEN   ☐ LITTLE MISS (please tick and order overleaf)

2 Door Hangers and Posters

PLEASE STICK YOUR 50P COIN HERE

In every Mr. Men and Little Miss book like this one, you will find a special token. Collect 6 tokens and we will send you a brilliant Mr. Men or Little Miss poster and a Mr. Men or Little Miss double sided full colour bedroom door hanger of your choice. Simply tick your choice in the list and tape a 50p coin for your two items to this page.

Door Hangers (please tick)
☐ Mr. Nosey & Mr. Muddle
☐ Mr. Slow & Mr. Busy
☐ Mr. Messy & Mr. Quiet
☐ Mr. Perfect & Mr. Forgetful
☐ Little Miss Fun & Little Miss Late
☐ Little Miss Helpful & Little Miss Tidy
☐ Little Miss Busy & Little Miss Brainy
☐ Little Miss Star & Little Miss Fun

Posters (please tick)
☐ MR.MEN
☐ LITTLE MISS

3 Sixteen Beautiful Fridge Magnets – any 2 for £2.00! inc.P&P

They're very special collector's items!
Simply tick your first and second* choices from the list below
of any 2 characters!

1st Choice

☐ Mr. Happy
☐ Mr. Lazy
☐ Mr. Topsy-Turvy
☐ Mr. Bounce
☐ Mr. Bump
☐ Mr. Small
☐ Mr. Snow
☐ Mr. Wrong

☐ Mr. Daydream
☐ Mr. Tickle
☐ Mr. Greedy
☐ Mr. Funny
☐ Little Miss Giggles
☐ Little Miss Splendid
☐ Little Miss Naughty
☐ Little Miss Sunshine

2nd Choice

☐ Mr. Happy
☐ Mr. Lazy
☐ Mr. Topsy-Turvy
☐ Mr. Bounce
☐ Mr. Bump
☐ Mr. Small
☐ Mr. Snow
☐ Mr. Wrong

☐ Mr. Daydream
☐ Mr. Tickle
☐ Mr. Greedy
☐ Mr. Funny
☐ Little Miss Giggles
☐ Little Miss Splendid
☐ Little Miss Naughty
☐ Little Miss Sunshine

*Only in case your first choice is out of stock.

--- TO BE COMPLETED BY AN ADULT ---

To apply for any of these great offers, ask an adult to complete the coupon below and send it with the appropriate payment and tokens, if needed, to MR. MEN OFFERS, PO BOX 7, MANCHESTER M19 2HD

☐ Please send _____ Mr. Men Library case(s) and/or_____ Little Miss Library case(s) at £5.99 each inc P&P
☐ Please send a poster and door hanger as selected overleaf. I enclose six tokens plus a 50p coin for P&P
☐ Please send me _____ pair(s) of Mr. Men/Little Miss fridge magnets, as selected above at £2.00 inc P&P

Fan's Name _____

Address _____

_____ **Postcode** _____

Date of Birth _____

Name of Parent/Guardian _____

Total amount enclosed £_____

☐ **I enclose a cheque/postal order payable to Egmont Books Limited**

☐ **Please charge my MasterCard/Visa/Amex/Switch or Delta account** (delete as appropriate)

Card Number

Expiry date ____/____ **Signature** _____

Please allow 28 days for delivery. We reserve the right to change the terms of this offer at any time but we offer a 14 day money back guarantee. This does not affect your statutory rights.

MR.MEN   LITTLE MISS
Mr. Men and Little Miss™ & ©Mrs. Roger Hargreaves

CUT ALONG DOTTED LINE AND RETURN THIS WHOLE PAGE